The Pout-Pout Fish
Goes to School

Deborah Diesen   Pictures by **Dan Hanna**

Farrar Straus Giroux   New York

For my writing group,
for teaching me —D.D.

To my wife, Jennifer—
a fintastic teacher
of little fish —D.H.

Farrar Straus Giroux Books for Young Readers
An imprint of Macmillan Publishing Group, LLC
175 Fifth Avenue, New York, NY 10010

Color separations by Embassy Graphics Ltd.
Printed in China by RR Donnelley Asia Printing Solutions Ltd., Dongguan City, Guangdong Province
First edition, 2014
10   9   8

mackids.com

Library of Congress Cataloging-in-Publication Data
Diesen, Deborah.
      The pout-pout fish goes to school : a Pout-pout fish adventure /
Deborah Diesen ; pictures by Dan Hanna. — First edition.
         pages cm
      Summary: Mr. Fish recalls how, on his very first day of school, he
anxiously went to one classroom after another watching students do
things he could not, until Miss Hewitt showed him to the room that was
right for beginners.
      ISBN 978-0-374-36095-5 (hardcover)
      [1. Stories in rhyme.   2. First day of school—Fiction.   3. Schools—Fiction.
4. Self-confidence—Fiction.   5. Fishes—Fiction.]   I. Hanna, Dan, illustrator.   II. Title.

PZ8.3.D565Pp 2014
[E]—dc23
                                                  2013001317

Farrar Straus Giroux Books for Young Readers may be purchased for business or promotional use.
For information on bulk purchases please contact Macmillan Corporate and Premium Sales
Department at (800) 221-7945 x5442 or by email at specialmarkets@macmillan.com.

A long time ago,
When Mr. Fish was very small,
He headed off to school
For the first time of all.

With a smooch from his parents,
And excited for his day,
Mr. Fish rushed in . . .
Then he lost his way!

S.S. Rock Bottom
Elementary School

The big fish around him
Knew exactly where to go,
Finding lockers, finding classes,
In a fast, smart flow.

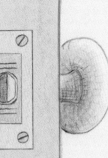

Mr. Fish, left behind,
With his grin sinking thin,
Finally stopped at a doorway
And he shyly looked in.

The class was doing writing,
And most everybody knew it.

So he tried to print his name . . .
But he just couldn't do it.

So he flub-flub frowned
Making blub-blub bubbles,
Then he plopped down his pencil
And he counted off his troubles:

"Trouble One: I'm not smart!

Trouble Two: I'll never get it!

Trouble Three: I don't belong!

So Four: I should forget it!"

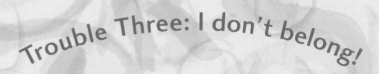

He floated with a frown
Down the long corridor,

Then he sneak-peeked a look
Through another room door.

The class was drawing shapes,
And most everybody knew it.

So he tried to make a rhombus . . .
But he just couldn't do it.

So he flub-flub frowned
Making blub-blub bubbles,
Then he plopped down his pencil
And he counted off his troubles:

"Trouble One: I'm not smart!

Trouble Two: I'll never get it!

Trouble Three: I don't belong!

So Four: I should forget it!"

He drifted down the hallway
With a doubt-doubt face,

Till he spied another doorway—
Maybe *this* was his place!

The class was doing math,
And most everybody knew it.

So he tried long division . . .
But he just couldn't do it.

So he flub-flub frowned
Making blub-blub bubbles,
Then he plopped down his pencil
And he counted off his troubles:

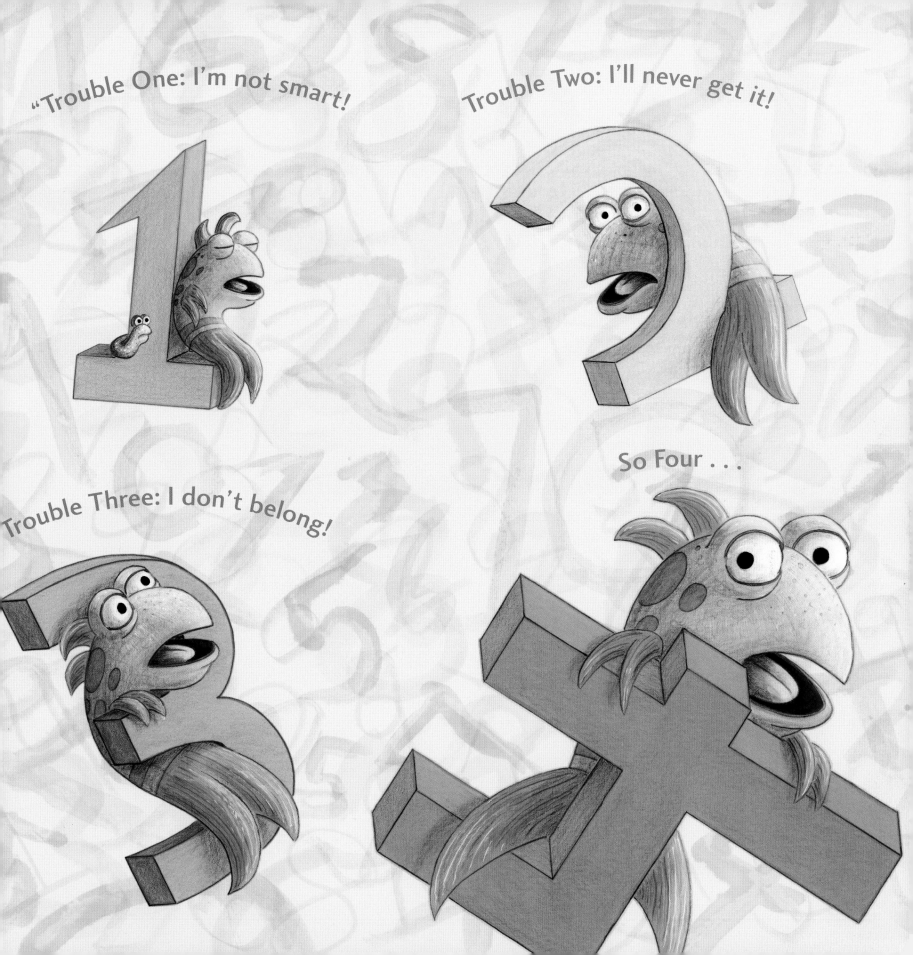

"FORGET IT!"

He rushed toward the exit.
"That's enough, I say!
School is way too tough,
And I'm *not* going to stay!"

Then a soft, kind voice said,
"Don't you fret!
You *don't* have to know things
You haven't learned yet!

"Your classroom awaits—
I'm your teacher, Miss Hewitt.
I am here to help you learn
And I know that you can do it!"

"You're a fish who is *smart*.
With practice, you will get it.
Young fish, you belong—
Don't you *ever* forget it!"

The student and the teacher
Swam a splish-splash swish
To a door with a sign
Marked BRAND-NEW FISH.

Miss Hewitt said, "Good morning!
I'm excited you're all here.
Together we will have
A spectacular year!

"Fact One: You are smart.
Fact Two: You can get it.
Fact Three: You belong.
So Four: Don't forget it!"

The class got to work,
And Miss Hewitt helped them through it.
They listened, then they tried . . .
And everyone could do it!

Mr. Fish gave a grin.
"Goodbye, blub-bubbles!
No more doubt-doubt worry!
No more flub-flub troubles!"

He swam with his class,
Miss Hewitt by his side,
As the students and their teacher
Said with confidence and pride:

"Fact One: We are smart!   Fact Two: We can get it!

Fact Three: We belong! And Four . . .

Clam Cam 2000